To Tiraya

Be all you can b

# FIRST STORY

*First Story changes lives through writing.*

We believe that writing can transform lives, and that there is dignity and power in every young person's story.

First Story brings talented, professional writers into secondary schools serving low-income communities to work with teachers and students to foster creativity and communication skills. By helping students find their voices through intensive, fun programmes, First Story raises aspirations and gives students the skills and confidence to achieve them.

For more information and details of how to support First Story, see www.firststory.org.uk or contact us at info@firststory.org.uk.

Lots of love
Grandad

People Are Not Poems
ISBN 978-0-85748-333-1

Published by First Story Limited
www.firststory.org.uk
Omnibus Business Centre,
39–41 North Road
London
N7 9DP



Typesetting: Avon DataSet Ltd
Cover Illustrator: Saqib Iqbal
Cover Designer: Lucy Dove
Printed in the UK by Aquatint

First Story is a registered charity number 1122939 and a private company limited by guarantee incorporated in England with number 06487410. First Story is a business name of First Story Limited.

# People Are Not Poems

## An Anthology

By The First Story Group
At Grange Technology College

Edited and introduced by Donavan Christopher | 2018

FIRST STORY
Changing lives through writing

‘We all have a voice. Some never discover it. We all have stories to tell. Some never tell them. First Story has helped all these young writers to discover their writing voice, and in so doing has helped them discover themselves.’
**Michael Morpurgo (author of *War Horse*)**

‘First Story is a fantastic idea. Creative writing can change people’s lives: I’ve seen it happen. It’s more than learning a skill. It’s about learning that you, your family, your culture and your view of the world are rich and interesting and important, whoever you happen to be. Teenagers are under increasing pressure to tailor their work to exams, and to value themselves in terms of the results. First Story offers young people something else, a chance to find their voices.’
**Mark Haddon (author of *The Curious Incident of the Dog in the Night-Time*)**

‘First Story not only does an invaluable thing for the young and under-heard people of England, it does it exceptionally well. Their books are expertly edited and beautifully produced. The students featured within are wonderfully open and candid about their lives, and this is a credit to First Story, whose teachers thoroughly respect, and profoundly amplify, their voices. The only problem with First Story is that they’re not everywhere – yet. Every young person deserves the benefit of working with them.’
**Dave Eggers (author of *A Heartbreaking Work of Staggering Genius*)**

‘First Story is an inspiring initiative. Having attended a school with a lot of talented kids who didn’t always have the opportunity to express that talent, I know what it would have meant to us to have real-life writers dropping by and taking our stories seriously. And what an opportunity for writers, too, to meet some of the most creative and enthusiastic young people in this country! It’s a joyful project that deserves as much support as we can give it.’
**Zadie Smith (winner of the Orange Prize for fiction and author of *White Teeth*)**

As Patron of First Story I am delighted that it continues to foster and inspire the creativity and talent of young people in secondary schools serving low-income communities.

I firmly believe that nurturing a passion for reading and writing is vital to the health of our country. I am therefore greatly encouraged to know that young people in this school – and across the country – have been meeting each week throughout the year in order to write together.

I send my warmest congratulations to everybody who is published in this anthology.

Camilla

HRH The Duchess of Cornwall

# Thank You

**Melanie Curtis** at **Avon DataSet** for her overwhelming support for First Story and for giving her time in typesetting this anthology.

**Vivienne Heller** for proofreading this anthology and supporting the project.

**Saqib Iqbal** for illustrating the cover of this anthology.

**Lucy Dove** for designing the cover of this anthology.

**Moya Birchall** at **Aquatint** for printing this anthology at a discounted rate.

**Arts Council England** for supporting First Story in this school.

**HRH The Duchess of Cornwall, Patron of First Story.**



**Thanks to**:
Arts Council England, Alice Jolly & Stephen Kinsella, Andrea Minton Beddoes & Simon Gray, The Anson Charitable Trust, The Arvon Foundation, BBC Children in Need, BBC Radio 4 Appeal &

Listeners, Beth & Michele Colocci, Big Lottery Fund, Blackwells, Boots Charitable Trust, Brunswick, Charlotte Hogg, Cheltenham Festivals, Clifford Chance, Danego Charitable Trust, First Editions Club Members, First Story Events Committee, Frontier Economics, Give A Book, Hollick Charitable Trust, Ink@84, Ivana Catovic of Modern Logophilia, Jane & Peter Aitken, John Lyon's Charity, John R Murray Charitable Trust, John Thaw Foundation, Lake House Charitable Foundation, Letters Live, Liz and Terry Bramall Foundation, Old Possum's Practical Trust, Open Gate Trust, Oxford University Press, Psycle Interactive, Robert Webb, Royal Society of Literature, Sigrid Rausing Trust, Sir Halley Stewart Trust, The Stonegarth Fund, Teach First, Tim Bevan & Amy Gadney, The Thomas Farr Charity, Walcot Foundation, Whitaker Charitable Trust, XL Catlin, our group of regular donors, and all those donors who have chosen to remain anonymous.

Most importantly we would like to thank the students, teachers and writers who have worked so hard to make First Story a success this year, as well as the many individuals and organisations (including those who we may have omitted to name) who have given their generous time, support and advice.

# Contents

# Introduction

Donavan Christopher

Writer-in-Residence

Creative writing is an art form of thoughts and ideas captured on paper. It's also a freedom of inner expressions, a free gift to all who choose to exercise it. A cohort of young writers at Grange Technology College took up this opportunity to explore and share their thoughts, ideas and writing techniques. This has been the third year of my residency at the school and it's been an honour to work with these new, young, enthusiastic students. We at First Story believe writing changes lives; this is always evident when a piece of writing is created. The excitement and confidence in students taking charge of this new-found freedom are a wonderful sight to behold.

The main outcome is for them to find their own voice and style. We are all driven by what we see and hear and can become almost a repeat: we are what we eat. Well, everyone has personal stories and experiences to share from their own life – everyone has their own spin on life. We all look but never see the same things until they're pointed out or found later by self-discovery. Travel is the same – we see, smell and taste a whole new world. To reflect, capture and recite the journey is what your material aims to do. You only have to write down the finer details – this will bring the reader into your world.

The group came together for sixteen weeks as Year Nine students from separate classes, quiet and seemingly shy. Over the first few sessions, breaking the ice and integrating the team, we played with words, created assumptions around pictures of people from the past, played quiz poetry and generally had fun. We made sure all were involved and everything was captured in their journals. They were also introduced to other authors – Nick Toczek and Amanda Whittington – who shared their knowledge and skills. I want to take a moment to thank them and let them know how invaluable they have been to our group. Some of the work done with these authors helped to shape this anthology.

Some students were producing some very interesting prose work and we could see confidence growing. The shift from not wanting to read to 'Please me, me!' is always a joy to see. The group were now entering First Story competitions and Team Grange were all delighted they were taking up the option. We were further amazed to hear one of our students had won a national competition. The whole group was excited and in disbelief, but it was a fact: we had produced a winner, which meant a win for all. This was reinforced when the group were invited to share their work at Chapel FM in Leeds.

I must say the students that attended the radio station were naturals, specifically when it came to sharing their work and projecting their voices. The host even asked one student to read a poem twice, as he loved the style of it. I'm sure you will find some amazing and interesting pieces in here that get you writing.

I must state this would never have been anything if First Story hadn't approached the school. If this is not changing lives through writing then let this collection be the start, as all these students can look back and see what they achieved at school away from the constraints of the curriculum. Some may go on to have their own books published; others, I hope, will continue to discover themselves. I wish them all the fortune they deserve, so they might further build up their confidence. Please remember this is where it started. Give them a platform, and support, and they will succeed in anything.

A final thank you to my main support team, Dianne Blashill and Austin Bradshaw, who have been the bridge of consistent surety and support between the students and me. Thanks again to the authors, who have offered lots of positive working practices at the writer and teacher meetings.

And finally a big shout of respect to the entire First Story team, who offered their professional support to produce this wonderful book of creative pieces.

# Foreword

Austin Bradshaw

TEACHER

I was introduced to the First Story programme when attending the launch of *Free at Last*, the anthology of poems produced by First Story's Grange students in 2017. I was very impressed by the standard of the work, and by the confidence of the young people reading their poems aloud to their teachers and family members.

Donavan Christopher was the poet-in-residence standing alongside them and encouraging them to take the stage. The two staff members who had worked with Donavan and the students to produce *Free at Last* were leaving the school that summer, so I quickly put myself forward to work alongside Dianne Blashill, the new librarian at Grange, to ensure the school would run the programme for another year with a new cohort of students.

I've not been disappointed.

Firstly, we have been lucky to work once again with Donavan, and the group of students who made a commitment to stick with the programme have been a joy to be with. The introductory workshop we ran in October 2017 emphasised that First Story was about participation, expressing oneself, and the chance for young people to be heard through their writing. Donavan also informed the students that while the workshops would be fun, we would be working towards producing writing of a high standard. I believe the twelve students who stayed with the programme to the end have succeeded in doing exactly that. We played a bit, used our imagination, shared our writing with each other and worked hard to get the best from our ideas.

Donavan's workshops were accessible and empowering for the students – a safe place, enabling them to be challenged and take risks with their writing. Subsequently, I witnessed a group of young people develop self-esteem and self-confidence, valuing their own and others' contributions in the workshops. Of course, the participants worked at different speeds, had different levels of ability and different experiences (for some students English is not their first language) but all found their voices in their poems and stories. I believe the creative potential of the group has been realised, and this is especially heartening as the curriculum and pressure of time in lessons is not conducive to students' artistic freedom or to developing their creative writing. I hope the First Story experience of seeing their work in print will encourage them to continue to be creative and keep writing. My thanks to them all, including Dianne, for participating in the production of this anthology, and to Donavan for sharing his expertise and energy.

# Foreword

Dianne Blashill

LIBRARIAN

This is the first year that I have been involved with First Story and my first year as librarian at Southfield Grange, and what a fabulous and busy year it has been.

First Story has given our students a wonderful experience – not just a chance to write and be published, but, through the opportunities it offers, the chance to meet different writers and broadcasters and to take part in a writing festival. One lucky student will be going on the residential writing experience at Lumb Bank.

When I was introduced to Donavan I assured him that I didn't write poetry, but his natural enthusiasm is so infectious that, by our second workshop, I found myself joining in with our students and thoroughly enjoying writing a poem – a first for me, as I've not written a poem since I was a scholar.

The number of students who were recommended by the English staff to be part of First Story ebbed and flowed, and by December we had a strong nucleus who were producing some amazing work. Their creativity has astounded me week after week. It has been interesting to see them grow from individuals who didn't know one another to a group of friends, sharing support and advice whilst bouncing ideas off one another, everyone shouting to be first to read their work out loud.

As well as working with Donavan Christopher, we have had visits from Amanda Whittington, playwright, and Nick Toczek, writer and magician, who introduced our students to different forms of writing, many examples of which are included in this anthology.

In March we took part in Writing on Air, an online literature festival hosted by Chapel FM, Leeds, where our students had the opportunity to broadcast their poetry – a first for most of us. It was exciting to go into a studio and be interviewed live on air; our students took live broadcasting in their stride and were focused and entertaining. Other 'firsts' have included a particularly shy member of the group finding his voice and insisting that he read a piece of work for our headmistress, Miss Mander. One of our writers is the 'school winner' of the First Story 100-Word Competition 2018 with her composition 'We're Not Poems', which became the basis for our choice of anthology title.

I'd like to thank everyone at First Story for their support, especially Andy Hill, who guided us through the mechanics of producing this anthology, and Camille Ralphs, who has displayed patience and given advice.

I'm grateful to Amanda who talked us through the rudiments of playwriting and characterisation. Thank you to Peter Spafford and colleagues from Chapel FM who made us feel so welcome in their amazing studio and performance spaces, showed us how a radio programme is put together, and issued an open invitation for us to go back and record another show. Saqib Iqbal produced the wonderful piece of artwork which graces the front of this anthology; as soon as I saw it I knew we had to have it. Thank you, Saqib, for helping out at the eleventh hour.

Thanks also to my colleague, Austin, who has put so much of his free time into helping our students produce the work contained in this anthology. Huge thanks must go to Donavan – he has (metaphorically) held mine and Austin's hands through our first experience of First Story, ensuring that we kept on the right track. His love of poetry and literature inspires and entertains past and present First Story students. The library bursts with poetry, rapping, laughter and plans whenever he visits.

There remains only one thing to say: 'May we do it all again next year?'

# We're Not Poems

Iqra Shahzad

Darling, people are not poems,
The rhythm and rhyme of a poem
Doesn't move like your body, nor arms;
The structure of them doesn't dance swiftly, like yours.
Like people, they are not edited –
Once they're published, they're gone.
You should know better,
My dear, once you've sprung out you'll understand
That people aren't always planned.
You'll see the beauty beyond yourself,
That you're more than what you have felt, but one thing,
Poems aren't always applauded, just like us,
But darling, just understand, poems are not people,
People are human and you're not perfect
Just precious and rare, not found everywhere.

# I Am...

Taseen Rehman

This is my alphabet with words that reflect
A personality that I accept
From A–Z as I reflect:

**A**spiring
**B**usy
And also **C**alm
**D**evoted
**E**ntertaining
**F**ragile and warm
**G**iant
**H**opeful
**I**ndecisive
**J**okester
A **K**ind
**L**oving and
**M**indful person
(checking things so they don't worsen)
**N**oisy
**O**bsessed
**P**ractical worker
**Q**uestioning
**R**acing
**S**ympathetic
**T**alker
**U**seful

**V**ocal
**W**riter
**X**iting
**Y**outhful
**Z**inging reciter!

# Double Trouble

Komal Iqbal

The creaking door opened to reveal two dark figures in the shrinking shadows,
Evil looks crawling across their faces like little spiders crawling around in the hot sun.
They were wearing matching clothes,
Guns placed on each side of their bright pink blazers.
Sweat started to drip down my hot, red cheeks,
My heart thumping as fast as an express train,
A clock just ticking louder and faster, like a cricket,
as the two evil twins stepped inside the door
and began to fidget.
I laughed hard!
Well, what should I expect from my best twin friends when we are invited to a costume party?

# The Box

Hanzala Shah

There it lay
With intimidation
Pulling me in like an electric ray.
It could be
An endless space of white and grey,
It could be
A world of beauty, peace and dreams.

Yet, once revealed,
Will it unleash a world
Which had once been concealed?
Will it unleash a world
Of forbidden horrors and death?
Not an item of happiness,
Not a sign of peace
But the brewer of wars.
It lay in front of me.

# Lucy Is a Bear

Robert Mennell

Lucy the bear has very long hair.
Her teeth are long and shiny, it's such a scare.
She can rip you in half with one claw
And destroy your stomach with one swipe of her paw
But she doesn't do that.
In fact
She will never attack –
She doesn't like doing that.
Instead, she will lick you and snuggle so fair
Because she's only a teddy bear.

# Time Traveller

Izza Asad

I witnessed battles that ended in floods of blood,
Blood that royalty called unclean,
Unclean, like the streets in Victorian times,
Times when the Egyptians ruled the lands,
Lands that Caesar conquered mercilessly,
Mercilessly Salem's men burning the witches,
Witches who told stories of prophecies and magic,
Magic spells protecting the Earth from destruction,
Destruction staining our timelines,
Timelines we learn from and improve.

# Lost and Found

Awais Zaib

Brian sat on the stool, lost in his thoughts, his face crinkled with distaste at what he had lost. He tried to fight the opposing memories by drinking another glass of wine, but the memories pulled him under. He was once famous. He was once known, but now resided in a broken-down pub on the edge of nowhere.

He started to reminisce about his last game, about how he had thundered down the pitch, leaving defenders dumbfounded in his wake. He had exerted force on the ball and it leapt up in the air. He had tapped the ball through the keeper's legs as it came down. He had helped score the winning goal in the World Cup finals. One moment of happiness, of joy, and the euphoria had leapt around him. He had felt like he could stand on top of the world.

Then the world came crashing down upon him.

The defender's intention was to take him down and Brian saw the player smile as he went for the tackle. Brian's leg gave way and the pain spread through him like a disease; he fell to the ground as the defender looked down at him. Brian's dream was shattered, his reality had gone in a flash.

Brian returned to the rowdiness of the pub. His face wrinkled with hurt as he felt tears welling up inside him. He tried to escape them but the voices and the stadium enveloped him again and again.

'You all right, mate?' the pub owner asked.

Bang! The snooker ball leapt off the table. Brian bounced it on to his leg, brought it up into the air for a header. For a time, he was lost in the zone – in this moment, the pain didn't come. This could be his new beginning. Brian's face, once covered with wrinkles, once wallowing, drowning in his own pain and sadness, was now shining out of the dark like a beacon of light.

# Mistakes Are Life's Fortunate Things

Ays Mohammed

Mistakes are life's fortunate things
And us to our destiny bring.
Good things can
Eventually
Come out of bad things.
Depression is the world's saddest emotion:
It can tear us all apart.
Strong emotions create a commotion
Of cause and effects.
Mistakes are life's fortunate things
We should live to expect.

# Six-Word Story

Komal Iqbal

Only giant chickens eat mini hamburgers.

A speedy mouse taking a nap.

A kid selling the biggest superstore.

# Religion

Taseen Rehman

Religion is a crazy place.
We all look before we taste.
Everyone feels free to believe in something.
Some people think it may be revolting.
Looking at others, then judging by colours;
Creating conflict, deceiving brothers.
In every home, there are many blessings,
But families are sometimes oppressing.
Blue eyes or dark-skinned,
We all see something –
In every mosque or church it is found,
Yet we all supress it, keep it in the background.
Only we decide what we see –
Either negligence or opportunity.
Religion is more than just a nation.
Look for the core of creation.

# The Inter-Dimensional Reality

Awais Zaib

Chicken fillet burgers that I eat from Salah's,
Salah, the Liverpool player who scores the winning goals in football,
Football that seems like a free-for-all,
A free-for-all like in *Fortnite Solo*, where you do quick scopes,
Quick scopes that are always on target like wizards,
Wizards who fight with magic instead of swords,
Swords that Future Trunks fights with against King Cold,
Cold the king, the leader of the tribe that conquers the universe,
The universe, a place of unimaginable wonders,
Wonders like chocolate that Willy Wonka creates out of nothing,
Nothing, from which came the Big Bang,
Bang, the sound heard when the ball hits its target,
Targets where Robin Hood lodges his arrows in the planet named Earth,
Earth, a home to a Greek god with a lightning bolt,
Bolting, the action of a Pokémon as it tries not to get caught in the Poké Ball,
The Poké Ball, in which Pikachu doesn't want to be trapped,
Trapped like Percy Jackson, Piper and Jason,
Jason, the friendly ghost that resides in the school called Grange,
Grange, a school where the library is a border to supernatural forces.

# Midnight Visit

Ays Mohammed

It was midnight, and I was exhausted after a hard day working on my farm. A flashing light forced my eyes to open. A creepy figure was glaring at me through the window. Its glowing eyes glittered neon in its dark skin. The window slowly opened but the figure had disappeared. I scrambled under my bed in an effort to hide from this monster; I could hear a whooooo-ooooh and I knew I wasn't alone…

I peeked from beneath the bed. I couldn't see the monster in the darkness – it was camouflaged against the velvet black of my bedroom. I crept slowly from my secret hiding place, I felt its presence, and I trembled knowing I wasn't alone.

Paralysis took over my muscles: I was rooted to the ground. Its long fingernails caught my arm, wrapping its rough ice-cold fingers around my biceps. I was lost…

# Call of Duty

Shaian Askari

Playing *Call of Duty*, got to survive,
Survival of the fittest, got to revive,
Revive my fellow friend, he's now in tears,
Tears show the emotions we feel,
Feel what's around us – sometimes large, sometimes small –
Small has no meaning when I'm feeling tall,
Tall and brave, weak and emotional,
Emotional feelings, we all need more –
More for the rich, less for the poor.
It's our call of duty, that's for sure.

# If You Are Struggling to Grow Up...

Halima Baig Noureen

This is night-time and I am trying to sleep,
But I am thinking about my dreams and hopes.
The room is filled with darkness and quietness.
The dreams are some moments of happiness –
If somebody wants to be happy, they should just think about
their dreams.
I am also so happy because I am thinking about my dreams.

# Do Great

Halima Baig Noureen

Do all the great deeds that you can.
Do all the good you know you can,
By all and any means you can,
By every major way you can,
In each and every day you can,
In all the places where you can,
Within all the smiles that you can.
Give as much time as you can
To all the people you know you can
As long and as forever as you can.
Because I know, and you know, that you can.

# Pandora

Taseen Rehman

The box lies in front of me,
Still and soundless,
Colours leaking from all four corners,
Creating light and happiness.
But when opened…
It will destroy and despoil,
Kill and claw
And end all life.
Its patterns and textures
Are so detailed,
Light to the touch
But grave to mankind.

The box lies in front of me.

# There Are Many Things That Make Me, Me

Shaian Askari

There are many things that make me, me,
Although there is one I can start with, my pride and joy,
The thing I've liked since I was a boy:
Chocolate, but not any old chocolate... Cadbury Cookie
Crumble.

But anyway, moving on to the things that really matter to me:
My family – they're always kind of happy –
and my sister's first steps.
We're really quite happy,
but not when it's Mum's turn to change the baby's nappy.

# Today's the Day I Truly Cried

Robert Mennell

Today's the day I truly cried
And there's nowhere to simply run and hide.
Believe me, folks, I tried
And four hours later, I nearly died.
I slipped on the floor, right on my side
And my tears came flooding like the tide.
I wasn't hurt, I said, I lied;
Something's in my eye, I implied,
But felt my mask finally starting to slide.
And that's the moment I truly cried.

# Test

Awais Zaib

I almost cried, trying to hide,
Escaping from the oncoming tide,
My face wide-eyed,
My mouth tongue-tied,
I sighed.

The ticking of the clock I was trying to abide
As I tried to divide.
My brain working frantically as it multiplied,
I pried through the contents of my mind.

The test is finished. I'm satisfied
Because I know I tried.

# Hardships

Izza Asad

Waves of emotions enclose you,
Overwhelm you and question your ambition.
The island which once seemed so close
Is suddenly an eternity away.

You wish to be swallowed by the ocean,
To be set free from the pressure,
But you are the only one who can provide protection.
You are the captain of this hardship.

Zip up your coat and laugh in the face of failure,
For ‘smooth seas do not make skilful sailors’.

# Surviving the Storm

Komal Iqbal

Storms are wild and uncontainable,
They can hurt,
They can be unexpected.
Storms seem to lock your heart and express your fear.

During a storm you would want to survive.
Go for it! Don't lose yourself in thought and waste your
precious time.
Batten down the hatches, pull in your sail –
Don't bother taking out time to rest or sit.
Make time for the things your teachers have taught you.

You will survive the storm!
Congratulate yourself with happiness
When the calm appears;
Don't let thunder or wind scare you,
Just let them blow away your fear.
Don't let yourself sit in sorrow and unhappiness.
Everything can change, just like the weather,
And even a storm can't last forever.

# Six-Word Autobiography

Ays Mohammed

Most mornings lead to messy hair.

This person is handsome, it's me.

# My Dreams

Robert Mennell

Oh! You would not believe me if I told you what happens in
my dreams.
Electronic, wacky and crazy are my dreams.
They're mean, lean and full of nicotine.
Do you really want to hear it? OK, here we go!
There's clowns in gowns, potatoes alive, books that can run and
cherries that are fun,
I scream fresh ice cream or any ice cream you want.
The teddies can talk,
Chairs can walk,
Bananas can fly, and sandwiches are flies.
My mum and dad sometimes appear with alien heads and covered
in toffee.
My dreams are as weird as the pimples on your neck,
They're sometimes pointless and make no sense.
They can be so intense,
But what the heck,
These are my dreams.

# Destiny

Taseen Rehman

The second my hand made contact with the old, cold silver knob, the door spoke to me. I tried to turn the stubborn silver, but it wouldn't budge. I reached into my pocket and searched for the worn-out key. I stood and swiftly inserted the key into the oak door. My emotions were scrambled as I turned the knob.

The door opened, and I could see my future; a lifeless reflection of myself. Tears started to fill my eyes. I found the letter I wrote just two weeks before and slipped it into my pocket.

I'd dreaded this day since it started.

# Life Is a Place of War

Ays Mohammed

Life is a place of war
War that ends up in blood
Blood that flows through our bodies
Bodies that help us live our lives
Lives that are suddenly taken away
Away to paradise
Paradise is a place of peace
Peace is a sanctuary of harmony
Harmony is the sound of music
Music that makes us sing and dance
Dance that brings us happiness
Happiness is an emotion of life

# The Beauty Called Imagination

Awais Zaib

Imagination is a journey you undertake,
A journey of battling minotaurs,
A journey to save a dying star,
A journey in a dystopian world,
A journey where brave mice battle the rats that try to lay siege to them,
A journey we all can take,
A journey we watch others make,
A journey of De Bruyne, sent from Chelsea to Man City,
A journey of his quest, our adventure
To watch him rise and become the best,
A knuckle ball wizard
On a journey with artistry
And all finding faith in the box.
Imagination is a box of unknown things –
How has it led you?

# The Chase

Jamal Tariq

My heart was beating like a drum as I ran helplessly through the forest. I glanced back to see a shadowy figure still following me, snapping twigs and ruining fallen leaves. My sight was blurred by the fog and the darkness of the night. A mixture of blood and sweat dripped down my face as fear overtook me like a disease. I came to a halt to catch my breath. Leaning against the tree, glancing back, I saw nothing but the fog devouring anything and everything from a distance.

# Six-Word Autobiography

Taseen Rehman

My pens, paper, notes, the future.

# Football

Awais Zaib

The glorious game.
Ronaldo, Messi, Neymar –
Players from different
backgrounds,
united in the same
game.
Fighting for their time
by pushing the opposition
back.
The goalkeeper parrying shot
after shot.
Gerrard comes up and
scores a stunner.
In the right corner,
Salah takes a shot
and de Gea saves
it spectacularly.

# Satisfied

Iqra Shahzad

Have you ever thought if you are fully satisfied?
You said you would work hard, but time has flied.
Now, you tried a lot but you have to decide –
You feel like you're emotionally dead inside,
Cold, lonely, and petrified?
Get back, back up again
And don't collide.
You should value trying, don't be denied.

Completion makes you satisfied
Because working hard will pay off the ride.
I'm just trying to say, 'Take some pride.'

When you have found that people have pushed you over,
Brush the dirt off your shoulder.

# If You Were a Soldier in World War I

Robert Mennell

The best of the best fought for our country
Who would have been forgotten if it wasn't for Wilfred Owen.
Our ancestors were proud.
Now it's time to speak out loud:
Stop annoying us with the same tales over and over again
Because we no longer 'believe the old lie'.
The blood's on your hands because of that silly lie –
How could you even make up such a disgusting lie?
Puddles of blood around the fields,
Shell shock and no shields.

If you were a soldier in the First World War,
Every day you'd miss your family a little bit more.
Your family and friends would miss you too
And there'd be nothing you could do,
Stuck in that damned trench,
Hoping to live another day.

At least you don't have to pay.
So be grateful to those who've gone,
To your great grandads and uncles
Who fought in World War I.

# We Are Worthy

Izza Asad

To Hell with people who live in the past –
The world is changing
And it's changing fast.
Don't you ever dare to surrender
And never be a fake pretender.

To be seen, to fight,
To protest, it is our right.
Our opinions deserve to be proclaimed –
The future demands to be explored and tamed.
Everything is in our hands and shall be explained.

Know your value,
Embrace your strength,
And, if they push you down,
Be sure to rebuild yourself
And rise back up stronger than before.
We are worthy.
I told you before.

# World of War

Ays Mohammed

War is everywhere.
Peace is nowhere.
Conflict is everywhere.
Happiness is somewhere.

Thus, we are survivors,
And we are defended
By all the heroes.
But has war ever ended?

# The Great Box

Komal Iqbal

In this box could be a journey of a lifetime.
Who knows where it might take you?
It could create different weathers or beautiful plants.
It could be the key to unlock your dreams.
What if it was a tool for a great magician, making peace
throughout the world?
What if there was a football pitch with mini people playing
inside the box?
What if there was a magic chocolate factory, creating magic
mini chocolate bars?
What if?
Should you open this box?
Its texture feels as smooth as a slippery fish but cold as Alaskan
steel.
Something so colourful and bright,
taking you into a magical land you have never imagined before.
The time has come.

# I Could Have Been...

Taseen Rehman

I could have been a hero,
I could have been a hero of lives,
I could have been a hero of minds,
I could have been a hero of all kinds.

I could have been the dream I dreamt,
I could have had a proper intent,
I could have made a brave ascent,
I could have been 100 per cent.
I could have been a fab creator,
I could have been the world's greatest baker,
I could have been a wildlife trapper,
I could have been an MC rapper.

We could have been great together,
But now I can't forget her.
How hard it was to actually get her.
I should have listened and should have read her.
I know I could have been much better.

# Return of Nosferatu

Hanzala Shah

Peeping through a curtain, I saw him for the first time. I looked because my curiosity took control of me. After all the threat of a storm, it hadn't started to rain, and was quite a pleasant night. Startled, I took one look at him and withdrew, my heart hammering loudly in my chest. If he hadn't seen me he would surely hear my magnifying heartbeat.

His eyes were two endless seas of black. His nose was curved, giving him an almost demonic look. His mouth was a leer. He frowned at the door as if waiting for it to open. I could almost smell the evil radiating from him. His clothes were not of our time. You don't get a lot of folk dressing up like that nowadays, and that is what finally made up my mind about not opening the door.

As quietly as I could, I turned and ran upstairs, where I hid for at least an hour.

But he was still in my head. His sunken eyes were as old as the sea itself. His cloak and clothes were worn down to exhaustion, like an old man sick of life. However, it was the jewel-encrusted dagger at his side that I kept seeing in my mind's eye. It was shiny and deadly, as if it had only been made yesterday, and I was sure it would not take long to skewer me and rip me to shreds.

Eventually, the compulsion to return got the better of me, and I went back down the stairs. I tugged cautiously at the curtain, only to see that he had disappeared. I let out a sigh of relief.

However, my joy was short-lived. I froze when, behind me, I

heard the scraping sound of metal against wood. The dagger against its scabbard.

My heart stood cold, my body frozen and still.

# The Box

Robert Mennell

Inside the box is a different world, a world named Leisure Land, where you can do anything imaginable. There are loads of colours everywhere, primary colours, dark shades and light pastels.

There is abandoned exercise equipment everywhere, as if it is a futuristic gym people have forgotten to visit.

The sun is made of chocolate which the people gorge upon.

The people inside this box are all alike: the girls resemble Marilyn Monroe and the guys channel Charlie Chaplin. The girls have itty bitty noses and the guys have giant bulging noses that make them look like Shrek. They conduct their conversations in gibberish. One of the guys once called me a veuxdjkdf*, by which I was offended. The girls are all in a cult worshipping Walt Disney and the boys all adore George Orwell's dystopian novellas. They treat me as a friend, and would never lay a finger on me, even though I think they act like weird freaks. They all live inside a huge square made of marble and gold.

Inside the box there is treasure scattered everywhere. Red jewels, gold jewels, blue jewels, gold bars, dollar bills and nickels galore are neatly piled, in order of worth.

There are watch chains and the anchors from the Titanic.

The Queen's head gear that she had to sell off to cover the debts incurred by excessive vet bills from her thirty Corgis.

A gold walking stick that Charlie Chaplin earned by playing the famous tramp who started the silent film era.

*The language of the KUEDX, from the gold star to the left of the Sun named Hollow Hole.

Purple gem bracelets and purple gem braces worn by Please Keyboards, the famous musician.

Cleopatra's gold teeth and Madonna's gold wig.

Elvis's gold guitars and Michael Jackson's deluxe edition CD. Hee Hee!!

Ten Hollywood gold-framed stars from ten different iconic film stars.

Magenta rocks.

Diana's tiara and Walt Disney's contract.

And much, much more, but that's another story. You'll have to discover for yourself if you find the box.

# The Coldness

Hanzala Shah

Cold. Darkness. Something violently slamming into my head. Losing consciousness, I fall into the darkness.

I wake and I'm instantly aware the room is moving. No, more like teleporting. Our speed is incredible. I stagger to the window and see stars and planets whizzing by.

That doesn't make sense? Here, there are stars.

Now it hits me – the ugly truth. I am being transported millions of miles away from my family. While I am lost in my thoughts, a door to my right opens and in steps an extremely strange creature. Its lower half is apelike, while its upper half is more human. Its head stretches back a full metre.

A jarring thud tells me we have landed and I attempt to barge past, but their speed is incredible. The creature tackles me to the ground and a coldness spreads throughout my body, numbing every muscle.

# Six-Word Story

Ays Mohammed

Whoever tells lies will endure pain.

# Where Hard Work Can Get You

Jamal Tariq

I'm on a Netflix trip on my phone,
Scrolling through the suggestions
As if they were telling people's life stories.
TV shows and movies show role models on air,
Making me wonder how they got there.

Actors telling stories through the actions of other personalities,
Footballers moving forward fast,
Basketball players flying high,
Businessmen expanding empires...

I see famous people come out of nowhere,
Moving on up, mastering their job.
I see students in college can become famous,
Athletes racing ahead, breaking and making records.

I'm using my remaining minutes
On inspiring people exceeding their limits,
Inspired to work hard.

# Exams

Ays Mohammed

Exams are tough and hard.
SATS were very easy,
GCSEs are written on cards.
Exams make me queasy.

You need a pass to get a job.
A job will get you money
To pay your bills, not be a slob.
To fail will not be funny.

In the end your exams
Should lead you to success.
Ignore the people who give you scams
And try not to get stressed.

# Loneliness

Jamal Tariq

What is loneliness?

Loneliness is the feeling you get when you're alone, no friends by your side, no family surrounding you and making you feel safe and comfortable – as if all the joy in you has been sucked out.

But then you feel like a wonder boy. With all this loneliness comes solitude, to think, to imagine, to create, to dream up incredible ideas to create impeccable machines, to make futuristic creations.

Loneliness does hurt, but it also can help – help to aspire, help to imagine, to imagine unimaginable things, unimaginable things that turn expectation into reality, dreams into reality.

# Friends

Komal Iqbal

All friends lead you in the right direction if they share a good connection.
True friends make you feel ecstatic because they are so truly fantastic.
No friends should ever lead you towards danger;
Loyalty and kindness are marks of a true Granger.
Some friends can be a bit ungrateful, even though they act so joyful.

My friends are the best – they're so inclined.
Each of them is delightfully refined.
Their love is complete and so divine;
Such precious stones are hard to find.

# Photograph of Somebody

Halima Baig Noureen

Her eyes are as light as the moon when I begin to take the photograph of Missi.

I see she's talked with somebody else – someone who hurts her. She is crying, such a sensitive girl. At this moment she looks like a crazy clown.

The sun is shining on her.

Suddenly, a shadow appears, and I am scared. But this is actually the shadow of Missi, because of the sunshine, the hot and warm days of summer.

Finally, she looks at me and smiles like a joker, and I take the picture of Missi.

# The Friendship

Halima Baig Noureen

One is my lover and one
Is her love.
It's my جذبہ
She is my truth,
She is my silliness,
She is the heartbeat in my heart
And never angry with me.
I pray for her.

جذبہ pronounced 'jasbah': your passionate feeling for someone; your best friend.

# Regret

Izza Asad

My heart pounded against my chest, begging to be released. My stomach turned itself inside out. It wasn't supposed to end like this. It wasn't supposed to end. Each step I took echoed throughout the hall but all I could hear was a high-pitched ringing in my ears. I glanced at my hands; they reflected the weakness of my mistake. Her door was growing larger as my heart made its way to my throat.

Her door creaked open. The silence was almost tangible. Her bloodshot eyes looked at me intently and promptly my spine transformed into ice.

# Six-Word Autobiography

Komal Iqbal

A girl flying in the air.

Loyal, kind, enthusiastic, that is me.

A crowded car travelling to France.

# Goodbye

Iqra Shahzad

My dear friend,
The time has come
Where we part our ways.
On different roads,
Oh friend,
Keep me near your heart
As our memories will never fall.
I know life is cruel, tearing us like a piece of paper,
But we shall meet again, my friend,
Because it is never really the end,
And paper can be glued back together again.
But not so, for a heart filled with pain.

# The Forgetful History Teacher

Donavan Christopher

Brethren, Romans,
Friends, friends, friends.
Enemies,
Brothers, sisters, citizens!
It has been brought to my attention!
Left, left, left, right March
Is such a beautiful time for daffodils
Are always placed in the hall
Where we usually do lots of exercise
Can be really good for your health
Problems should be avoided to live a long life
This can also be very hard,
Boiled eggs are not to be fried.
Rice, chicken with bits of batter, and tomato sauce
Of energy
Can be restored by eating
Healthily.
Now what was I saying, now I remember, friends, enemies, citizens.

# Neglect

Donavan Christopher

Everybody looking for solutions.
Statistics, facts, analytical conclusions.
Ballistic acts, political intrusions.
Words spoken, people misguided.
Wealth and dowry
Nonchalantly divided,
The fate of nations already decided.

No one knows or understands
How deep the wounds are from oppression.
Who feels it knows it, they know they never chose it.

Never been accepted whilst always felt subjected
When pride has been scolded
And even cold-shouldered,
Futures being moulded, lives already corroded.

Only the strong survive; some would rather die
Than be a slave, never feeling free
Whenever they hear democracy,
For someone's dream of immortality,
Destroying people's lives and mentality.

Problems caused, out comes brutality.
Reactions are caused, out comes fatality.
Solutions are made their scheme of reality.